Life in Freshwater Marshes

BY MIRELLA S. MILLER

Published by The Child's World®
1980 Lookout Drive • Mankato, MN 56003-1705
800-599-READ • www.childsworld.com

Acknowledgments
The Child's World®: Mary Berendes, Publishing Director
Red Line Editorial: Editorial direction
The Design Lab: Design
Amnet: Production

Design Elements: Eric Isselee/Shutterstock Images; Vadim Petrakov/Shutterstock Images

Photographs ©: Warren Price Photography/Shutterstock Images, cover (center), 1 (center); Eric Isselee/Shutterstock Images, cover, 1; Vadim Petrakov/Shutterstock Images, cover, 1 (repeating); Brian Lasenby/Shutterstock Images, 4–5; Francesco de Marco/Shutterstock Images, 7; Mogens Trolle/Shutterstock Images, 8; Spirit of America/Shutterstock Images, 10–11; Shutterstock Images, 13, 19, 21; Sergey Uryadnikov/Shutterstock Images, 14; Super Prin/Shutterstock Images, 17; Tatiana Volgutova/Shutterstock Images, 21 (top); Roger de Montfort/Shutterstock Images, 21 (middle); Raffaella Calzoni/Shutterstock Images, 21 (bottom)

ISBN 9781626872967
LCCN 2014930650

Printed in the United States of America
Mankato, MN
July, 2014
PA02218

ABOUT THE AUTHOR

Mirella S. Miller is an author and editor from Minnesota. She hopes to visit the Everglades someday.

CONTENTS

Welcome to a Marsh

It is morning in a marsh. The rising sun shines on the water. Tall grasses bend with the wind. Dragonflies buzz around the cattails. A heron flies over the water. An alligator's eyes pop above the

water's surface. He looks around for food. He is hungry.

This freshwater marsh is a water biome. A biome is a place in nature that supports certain types of life. Plants and animals of a biome are specially suited to live there. Let's learn more about freshwater marshes!

Everglades National Park is in Florida.

What Is a Marsh?

A marsh is a type of wetland. Wetlands are areas of land covered by **shallow** water. There are many types of wetlands. Some wetlands have salty water. Others have freshwater. This means there is no salt in the water. Most marshes contain freshwater.

Marsh water is not deep. It is usually from 1 foot (0.3 m) to 6 feet (1.8 m) deep. Freshwater marshes are found in low, open areas. They are near shallow lakes and the mouths of some rivers. This is where the river flows into another body of water. Marshes are located around the world.

Many plants and animals live in freshwater marshes. Different types of grasses grow well. Very few trees are found. Other plants and rice grow in marshes. Insects, birds, deer, and other animals live by marshes, too.

An American bittern bird blends in with marsh grasses.

A Marsh Forms

Freshwater marshes form near the edges of bodies of water. The water from streams, rivers, and lakes flows into marshes. More water makes a bigger marsh. The water level changes during a year.

The Okavango River empties into a large marsh.

The Okavango Delta in Botswana is one of the largest freshwater marshes in the world. It is approximately 5,800 square miles (15,000 sq km).

Sometimes a marsh floods. This happens when too much water flows into the area. Marshes also dry out. In the spring, they fill up again as water flows in.

There are many sizes of marshes. Some are small. They form along the edges of lakes. Others are big, like the Everglades in Florida. Lake Okeechobee and the Kissimmee River flow into the Everglades.

The soil drains slowly near marshes. It is full of **minerals**. Plants use the minerals to grow. Dead plants **decay**. They become food for different animals.

Marshes may have wet and dry seasons. Animals that live in marshes move during the dry season. They find other places near water. These animals return during the wet season.

Types of Marshes

There are two types of marshes. One type is a tidal marsh. This marsh is found along ocean coasts. There are many tidal marshes along the East Coast of the United States. Tidal marsh water levels change during the day. The water moves in and out with ocean tides. Some tidal marshes have freshwater, while others have saltwater.

The Rachel Carson Wildlife Refuge is a tidal marsh along Maine's coast.

Non-tidal marshes are common in North America. These marshes have only freshwater. They are found near rivers and lakes. The Everglades is the largest non-tidal marsh in the United States. Non-tidal marshes have good soil and many plants. These plants provide homes for many types of animals.

Alligators in the Everglades

Everglades National Park is on the southern tip of Florida. The park is made of many small marshes. They create a large marsh area. The park's marshes cover more than 4,300 square miles (11,100 sq km). The water is thick with saw grass. Birds, insects, and other animals live in the grass. One of the most common animals is the alligator.

Alligators are large reptiles. They can grow up to 19 feet (6 m) long. They spend most of their lives in freshwater. Alligators use their strong tails to move through the water. They are fast swimmers. This helps them catch their **prey**.

Alligators eat fish, birds, and small mammals. With 80 teeth, it is easy for alligators to catch food.

More than 100 types of marsh plants grow in the Everglades. Saw grass is the most common.

Then they swallow their food whole. Alligators hunt at night. Their eyes, ears, and noses are on the tops of their heads. Their large bodies hide under the water.

Alligators dig holes in the marsh dirt where they rest. Female alligators build nests and lay eggs. They use grass and mud to make the nests. Then they use the thick marsh grass to hide the nests. Female alligators guard their nests from **predators**. Panthers, snakes, and birds try to eat the eggs.

Alligators have bony plates that cover their backs.

In the Marsh

Marshes have three **zones**. The zones are underwater, on the water's surface, and at the marsh's edges. Different plants and animals live in each zone.

Plants are important to marsh biomes. Grasses are the most common plants. Marsh grass is a strong,

Muskrats have webbed feet to help them swim.

Female muskrats can have up to 30 babies in one summer.

tall plant. It grows in clumps. Some kinds grow up to 10 feet (3 m) tall. Marsh grass grows in North America, Africa, and Europe.

Marsh grasses are home to muskrats. These animals are the smaller cousins of the beaver. They use grass and mud to make lodges. Muskrats feed on the roots and stems of grasses and other plants. They also eat clams and snails.

Because water levels change in marshes, there are few fish that live in the water. Northern pike and carp live in deep marshes. They feed on dead plants and worms.

Above the Marsh

A marsh's surface is also filled with life. Floating plants drift between thick grasses. **Photosynthesis** happens here.

Water lilies and lotuses are two kinds of floating plants. Both plants have flowers. The flowers attract insects. They feed on the flowers' nectar. Frogs hop from lily pad to lily pad. Fish and other animals eat the plants' stems below water.

Red-winged blackbirds, great blue herons, and ducks visit marshes. Red-winged blackbirds land on cattails and tall grasses. Ducks swim in the water. They dive below the surface to catch food. Great blue herons nest in the grasses. They hunt fish and frogs.

Nearby trees often fall in marsh water. These fallen or dead trees become homes for many animals. Turtles and snakes lay in the sun on tree trunks. Great blue herons rest on the trees. Raccoons use fallen trees as hunting spots. They look for frogs.

A moorhen uses a lotus pad as a perch.

Around the Marsh

The area around a marsh is the last zone. This includes the shoreline. Many plants and trees grow in this zone. Larger animals live in this area, too. Some animals just visit the marsh for food or water.

Bulrush plants grow along the shore. These plants are tall grasses. They have clumps of spikes at the top. Bulrushes help clean the water. Cattails also grow along the shore. These are **reed** plants. These plants have brown, furry tops. They grow in mild and cold regions around the world.

Different animals live near the edges of marshes. Marsh deer live in South America. They are good swimmers. Marsh deer hide in the grass from jaguars. They also eat the grass. The Everglades are home to Florida panthers. They hunt in the morning and at night. Panthers eat white-tailed deer, raccoons,

There are an estimated 100 to160 panthers living in South Florida.

and birds. The Okavango Delta has many different animals. Hippopotamuses, crocodiles, giraffes, and elephants stop for water.

Marsh deer live in the Ibera swamps of Argentina.

The Marsh Food Chain

Marshes are home to many plants and animals. Each plant and animal is important to the marsh's food chain. This is the way that plants and animals work together in a habitat.

A marsh's food chain starts with sunshine. Marsh plants use the sun's energy to grow. The marsh's soil gives **nutrients** to the plants. Raccoons and marsh deer feed on the plants. Alligators eat muskrats and other small animals. Fish and birds also become food for larger animals.

Each plant and animal is important to a freshwater marsh biome. When living things work together, it makes a healthy home. Marshes would not be the same if one plant or animal was missing.

In one kind of marsh food chain, grasses use the sun's energy to grow, muskrats eat grass, and alligators eat muskrats.

GLOSSARY

decay (di-KAY) To decay is to rot or break down. Plants decay into marsh soil.

minerals (MIN-ur-uhls) Minerals are natural substances in the ground, such as salt. Marsh soil contains many minerals.

nutrients (NOO-tree-uhnts) Nutrients are something plants and animals need to stay alive and healthy. Water that settles in marsh soil gives plants nutrients.

photosynthesis (foh-toh-SIN-thi-sis) Photosynthesis is the process plants use to convert sunlight into food energy. Marsh plants use photosynthesis.

predators (PRED-uh-turz) Predators are animals that hunt other animals for food. Alligators guard their nests from predators.

prey (PRAY) Prey are animals that are hunted for food by other animals. Alligators use their teeth to catch their prey.

reed (REED) A reed plant is a tall grass that has stems and grows in or near wet areas. Cattails are a reed plant.

shallow (SHAL-oh) Shallow water has little depth. Marshes have shallow water.

zones (ZOHNS) Zones are areas set off from surrounding parts. Marshes are made up of three zones.

TO LEARN MORE

BOOKS

Leotti-Bachem, Janice. *Everglades*. New York: Children's Press, 2009.

Watson, Galadriel. *Wetlands.* New York: Weigl Publishers, 2006.

Zobel, Derek. *Alligators*. Minneapolis: Bellwether Media, 2012.

WEB SITES

Visit our Web site for links about the freshwater marsh biome:

childsworld.com/links

Note to Parents, Teachers, and Librarians: We routinely verify our Web links to make sure they are safe and active sites. So encourage your readers to check them out!

INDEX